ESTHER'S RAINBOW

Kim Kane & Sara Acton

ALLEN&UNWIN
SYDNEY · MELBOURNE · AUCKLAND · LONDON

For
Polly
S.A.
x

For George
who first saw
the rainbow
and for Edgar
who dreamt
it.   K.K.

One Sunday, Esther was eating lunch
when she spied a rainbow.

Its tip was poking just under her stool.

Esther leant down to touch it.
It was soft.
It was warm.
And it smelt slightly like honey.

Esther's rainbow hummed a secret hum.
It slid over her fingers.
Then, as quickly as it had come, it was gone.

That night at dinner, Esther peeked under her stool.
The floor was cold.

On Monday, Esther saw **violet**
in Daddy's work-pressed shirt,
in a bruise on her shin,
in chalk on the kitchen blackboard
and in the velvet of the good couch.

She tasted **violet** in Granny's chocolate creams…

but she couldn't find her rainbow.

On Tuesday, Esther saw **indigo**
in a wonky hat,

on a forgotten feather,

in nail polish,
hard and shiny.

She smelt **indigo** in the cool of the midnight sky…

but she couldn't find her rainbow.

On Wednesday, Esther saw **blue**
in the buttons on Mummy's cardigan,
in the tiny face of a forget-me-not,

in her brother's swim-cold lips
and a towel wrapped around
his shoulders tight.

She heard **blue**
in the echo of the pool ...

but she couldn't find her rainbow.

On Thursday, Esther saw **green**
in bottles glinting in the bin,

in fishpond slime,

on a traffic light
and Danny's proud two-wheeler.

She smelt **green** in mint, crushed between her fingertips...

but she couldn't find her rainbow.

On Friday, Esther saw **yellow**
in the sticky yolk of her googy-egg,

on baby's I-like-butter chin,

on a safety vest, the swing seat
and Daddy's taxi home.

She felt **orange** between her fingers as they dug deep into clay ...

but she couldn't find her rainbow.

On Sunday, Esther saw **red**
in raspberry ice,

in the warm bricks
of the garden wall,

in the fins of a fish

and the ruby-seeds of a pomegranate.

She smelt **red** in Granny's roses...

but she couldn't find her rainbow.

The next day was Monday again.
Esther woke to a rain shower, soft and sweet and new.

She woke to pancakes curling in the pan.
She woke to a long, low honey-hum.

Esther spied her rainbow
in the corner of the mirror.

The hum grew.

Esther spied her rainbow on a bubble in the sudsy sink
and in the eye of Mummy's opal ring.

The hum grew louder still.

Then she saw it . . .

Arching over her garden,
bright and majestic, loud and long.

Singing as deep and violet as a bruise,
singing as sweet and golden as butter.

Esther's rainbow.

A rainbow to sing her own.

A rainbow that still smelt
slightly like honey.

Allen & Unwin
83 Alexander Street
Crows Nest NSW 2065
Australia
Phone: (61 2) 8425 0100
Email: info@allenandunwin.com
Web: www.allenandunwin.com

A Cataloguing-in-Publication entry is available
from the National Library of Australia
www.trove.nla.gov.au

ISBN 978 1 76011 337 7

Cover & text design by Ruth Grüner
Set in 20 pt Granjon by Ruth Grüner
Colour reproduction by Splitting Image, Clayton, Victoria
This book was printed in January 2015 at Hang Tai Printing (Guang Dong) Ltd.,
Xin Cheng Ind Est, Xie Gang Town, Dong Guan, Guang Dong Province, China.

1 3 5 7 9 10 8 6 4 2